GO, Gabbie, GO!

Hollie Noveletsky

Illustrated by Gabrielle Studley

Tellwell Talent
www.tellwell.ca

ISBN
978-0-2288-8818-5 (Hardcover)
978-0-2288-8817-8 (Paperback)

This book is dedicated to
Gabrielle 'Gabbie' Studley, my friend and illustrator.

Always follow your dreams!

With a great big smile, Gabbie spread her arms wide, put her face to the wind, and flew high into the sky. Or at least... Gabbie flew high for a few seconds as she jumped off a tall rock before landing gently on the grass. Gabbie wanted to fly more than anything. She wanted to soar in and out of the big white puffy clouds as they sailed across the sky. She wanted to fly low along the winding rivers and up over the steep mountaintops.

At night, Gabbie would lie across her bed with her chin on the windowsill, her nose pushed up tight against the cool windowpane, staring in wonder at the star-filled sky. Gabbie dreamed of flying among the stars. She wanted to see how beautiful the night world looked from above. Gabbie gently closed her eyes and pictured the twinkling lights of the cities and towns below.

As the morning sunshine broke through Gabbie's bedroom window, she stretched her arms wide and yawned a great big yawn. Then, Gabbie jumped out of bed and grabbed her brown leather aviator hat, her goggles, and her cream-colored scarf. She put on her aviator hat and adjusted her goggles. As she wrapped the scarf around her neck, Gabbie wondered aloud: "Who should I fly with today?" And with a final toss of the scarf over her shoulder, she was off for an adventure.

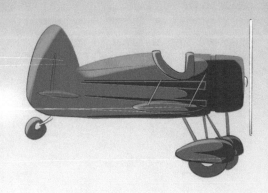

Pancho Barnes

Gabbie loved to pretend to fly with all the famous women pilots who ever lived. Gabbie would fly around her backyard, across the stream, over the rocks, and through the field with the best of the best by her side. Today, Gabbie decided to fly with the world-famous woman stunt pilot, Pancho Barnes.[1] Gabbie spread her arms wide and put her nose to the wind as she and Pancho Barnes took off. They taxied down the grassy runway and gently lifted off into the sky. Gabbie, with Pancho Barnes by her side, flew slow rolls, loop-the-loops, and figure eights back and forth across her yard. They flew, and they flew, and they flew some more. They flew until Gabbie's arms were so tired that she could hardly hold them up anymore.

Pancho Barnes was an American aviator (July 22, 1901–March 30, 1975).

[1] Hume, Ellen. "'Pancho' Barnes, Woman Pilot, Dies." *Los Angeles Times*, 30 March 1975, p. B5.

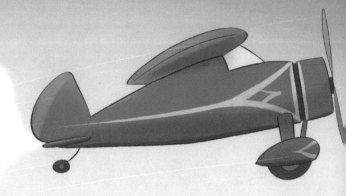

Amelia Earhart

After a quick peanut butter and jelly sandwich and a cold glass of milk in Gabbie's airport cafe, Gabbie was ready to fly again. Gabbie spied the little stream crossing her yard and she knew that it was an adventure for Gabbie and Amelia Earhart[2] to fly. After all, Amelia Earhart was the first woman to fly solo across the Atlantic Ocean. Gabbie straightened her aviator hat and adjusted her goggles as she started toward the runway with Amelia Earhart by her side. They taxied down the grassy runway and gently lifted off into the sky. Gabbie and Amelia flew across the great stream from North America to Europe. They crisscrossed the stream, landing in North America and Europe again and again and again until, finally, Gabbie and Amelia decided their mission was complete. They turned their plane into the wind and rolled down the grassy runway.

Amelia Earhart was an American aviator (July 24, 1897 – disappeared July 2, 1937).

2 Pearce, Carol A. Amelia Earhart. *Facts on File*. 1988

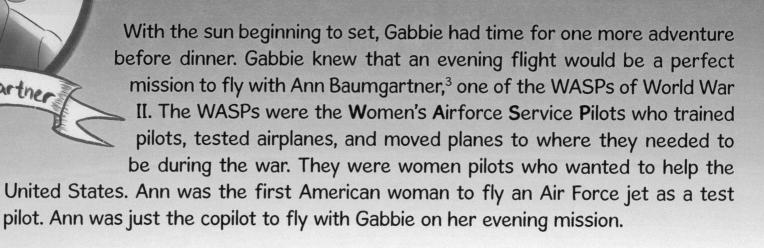

Ann Buamgartner

With the sun beginning to set, Gabbie had time for one more adventure before dinner. Gabbie knew that an evening flight would be a perfect mission to fly with Ann Baumgartner,[3] one of the WASPs of World War II. The WASPs were the **W**omen's **A**irforce **S**ervice **P**ilots who trained pilots, tested airplanes, and moved planes to where they needed to be during the war. They were women pilots who wanted to help the United States. Ann was the first American woman to fly an Air Force jet as a test pilot. Ann was just the copilot to fly with Gabbie on her evening mission.

Gabbie and Ann taxied down the grassy runway and gently lifted off into the sky. They flew fast and low, following the ground. Gabbie and Ann flew low over the field, then high over the rocks, and then low again over the stream. After one last fast pass over the field, Gabbie and Ann headed for the runway. Dinner was waiting...

Ann Baumgartner was an American aviator (August 27, 1918 – March 20, 2008).

[3] "FLYING FOR FREEDOM The Story of the Women Airforce Service Pilots." (PDF). Teacher Resource Guide. United States: National Museum of the United States Air Force. Archived from the original (PDF) on 26 December 2010.

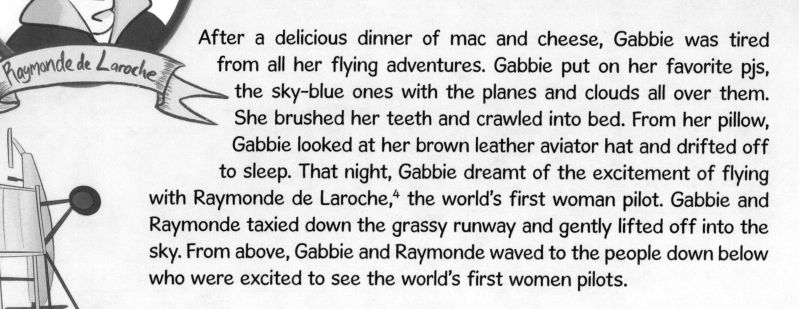

Raymonde de Laroche

After a delicious dinner of mac and cheese, Gabbie was tired from all her flying adventures. Gabbie put on her favorite pjs, the sky-blue ones with the planes and clouds all over them. She brushed her teeth and crawled into bed. From her pillow, Gabbie looked at her brown leather aviator hat and drifted off to sleep. That night, Gabbie dreamt of the excitement of flying with Raymonde de Laroche,[4] the world's first woman pilot. Gabbie and Raymonde taxied down the grassy runway and gently lifted off into the sky. From above, Gabbie and Raymonde waved to the people down below who were excited to see the world's first women pilots.

Raymonde de Laroche was a French aviator (August 22, 1882– July 18, 1919).

[4] Eileen F. Lebow. Before Amelia: Women Pilots in the Early Days of Aviation. *Brassey's*. p. 14. 2003.

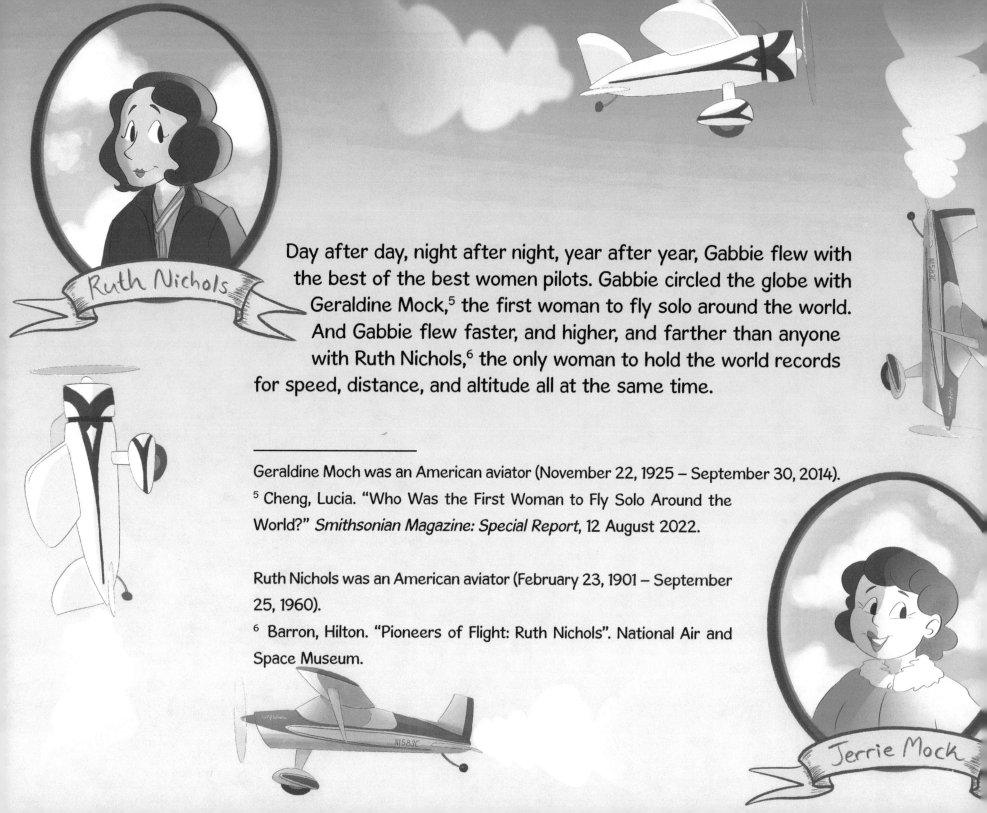

Day after day, night after night, year after year, Gabbie flew with the best of the best women pilots. Gabbie circled the globe with Geraldine Mock,[5] the first woman to fly solo around the world. And Gabbie flew faster, and higher, and farther than anyone with Ruth Nichols,[6] the only woman to hold the world records for speed, distance, and altitude all at the same time.

Geraldine Moch was an American aviator (November 22, 1925 – September 30, 2014).

[5] Cheng, Lucia. "Who Was the First Woman to Fly Solo Around the World?" *Smithsonian Magazine: Special Report*, 12 August 2022.

Ruth Nichols was an American aviator (February 23, 1901 – September 25, 1960).

[6] Barron, Hilton. "Pioneers of Flight: Ruth Nichols". National Air and Space Museum.

Jeannie Leavitt

And Gabbie flew dangerous missions with Jeannie Leavitt,[7] the first woman fighter pilot in the U.S. Air Force.

Major General Jeannie Leavitt (born 1967) is an American aviator and officer in the U.S. Air Force.

[7] "First female fighter pilot becomes first female wing commander." *Fox News*. 31 May 2012.

Gabbie Studley

Finally, after all those days and nights and years of flying with the best of the best women pilots, it was Gabbie's turn to take her place alongside of them. Gabbie had studied hard, read all her manuals, and passed all her written tests. And today was the BIG DAY! Today was the day Gabbie had worked so hard for. Today was the day Gabbie got to fly solo in a real airplane.

Gabbie grabbed her new blue aviator jacket, tied her cream-colored scarf around her neck, and pulled on her brown leather aviator hat and goggles. Gabbie began to smile as she crossed the field to her plane. By the time Gabbie reached the plane, her smile was so big that her face began to ache.

Gabbie Studley

Gabbie climbed up into the plane. A rush of excitement ran through Gabbie from her hair to her toes as she grabbed the stick. Gabbie took a long, slow, deep breath. As Gabbie exhaled, she quietly said, "Solo at last!" Gabbie took another long, slow, deep breath and started the engine. *Sput, sput, sput...* and then the propeller started to spin faster and faster. Gabbie pushed the throttle forward and taxied the plane to the runway. With a smile from ear to ear, Gabbie pushed the throttle forward more and the plane began to lift into the air. As the plane climbed up into the sky, Gabbie was sure she heard a chorus of familiar voices shouting to her, "Go, Gabbie, go!"

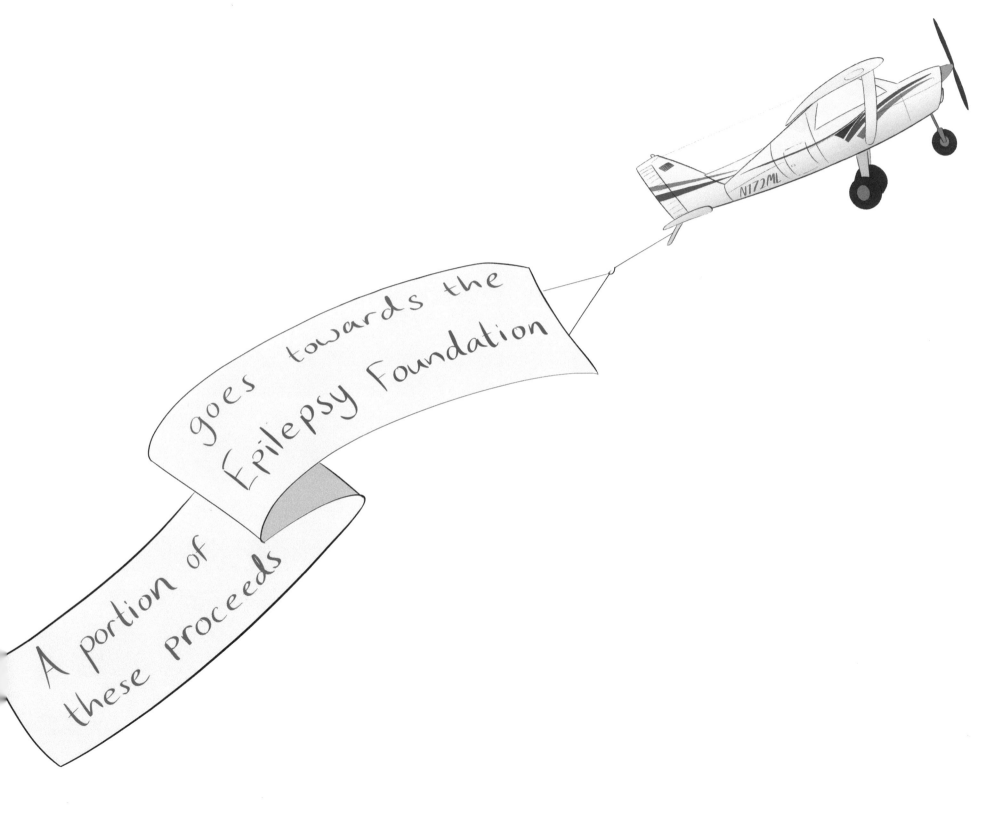